This book belongs to:

....

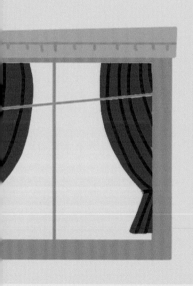

For Marie, London forever! - MB

First published 2023 by Campbell Books,
an imprint of Pan Macmillan
The Smithson, 6 Briset Street, London EC1M 5NR
EU representative: Macmillan Publishers Ireland Ltd,
1st Floor, The Liffey Trust Centre, 117-126 Sheriff
Street Upper, Dublin 1, D01 YC43
Associated companies throughout the world
www.panmacmillan.com

ISBN: 978-1-0350-2173-4

Text and design © Macmillan Publishers
International Limited 2023
Illustrations © Marion Billet 2023

A CIP catalogue record for this book is available from the British Library

Printed in the UK

FSC
www.fsc.org

MIX
Paper | Supporting
responsible forestry
FSC® C116313

KING CHARLES III's
COLOURFUL
CORONATION

Marion Billet

King Charles the Third jumped out of bed,
Wiggled his toes and then he said,

Woof!

Woof!

"I must get **dressed** without delay.
Today's my coronation day!"

In **long** red **robes**, he joined his **guard**,
Who stood in **rows** out in the **yard**.

He hopped in his coach and shouted,
"March! Down the Mall and round the arch."

The crowds nearby cheered, "HOORAY!
King Charles the Third is on his way."

Until . . .

"STOP the coach!" King Charles said.

"Let's meet those people up ahead."

Builders in orange called, "Good day!"

Then King Charles went on his way.

Until . . .

"STOP the coach! Please mind that fellow.

It's a lollipop man dressed in yellow."

The **lollipop man** said, "STOP!" then "GO!"
And off the coach rolled, nice and slow.

"STOP the coach, I'd like to meet,
Everyone along the street."

First, King Charles was very keen,
To greet nurses dressed in green.

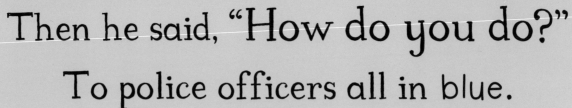

Then he said, "How do you do?"
To police officers all in blue.

And, finally, he waved, "Hello!"

To pearly kings in indigo.

By then, a party had begun,
And King Charles met EVERYONE.

There were violet flags, balloons and cake.

He stopped for tea and took a break.

Soon, King Charles was very late,
"Back to the coach! We cannot wait."

He ran past people **big** and small,
And waved **hello** to one and all.

Then in a flash, his gold coach sped.
"To the Abbey!"
King Charles said.

They reached **Westminster** just in time,
To hear the **noisy** church bells **chime**.

King Charles was crowned and what a sight!

His rainbow jewels shone **big** and **bright**!

The crowd waved flags in red, white and blue,
Sang songs and cheered – and some cried, too.

"Long live the King!"

"Hip-hip-hooray!"

"Happy coronation day!"

Charles called, "I'm proud to be your king.
Thank you all for everything."

I wear my red Robe of
State when I arrive at
Westminster Abbey.
Then I promise
to serve my country
and The Commonwealth.

This golden robe is
the Supertunica.
I wear it while I hold
special objects
that represent my
important responsibilities.

When I leave my coronation,
I wear my violet Imperial Robe
and a new crown, called
The Imperial State Crown.
It's so heavy that I can't look down
or it will fall off!

The crown jewels are
all precious and important
to me. Which is your
favourite?

First, I hold the sparkly Sovereign's Orb in my right hand. It is covered in emeralds, rubies, sapphires, diamonds and pearls!

Then, I hold two sceptres. This one is called The Sovereign's Sceptre with Cross. The diamond at the top is the biggest of its kind in the world!

Finally, I am crowned with the St Edward's Crown. It is the most important crown of all and it is 362 years old!